Princess Polly to the Rescue

Poor Prince Tom has been captured by Haggis the witch.

'I don't suppose if we just left Prince Tom to it, he could rescue himself?' asks Princess Polly.

'No chance,' replies Tom's godfather, Wizard Idea.

And so, helped by the Magic Bird, Polly sets out on an exciting journey to save the Prince . . .

MARY LISTER

Princess Polly
to the Rescue

Illustrated by Ron Hanna

A Magnet Book

For my children, Tom and Polly

First published in Great Britain 1984
by Methuen Children's Books Ltd
This Magnet edition first published 1986
by Methuen Children's Books Ltd
11 New Fetter Lane, London EC4P 4EE
Text copyright © 1984 Mary Lister
Illustrations copyright © 1984 Ron Hanna
Printed in Great Britain by
Richard Clay (The Chaucer Press) Ltd
Bungay, Suffolk

ISBN 0 416 00572 1

Contents

1
Haggis' Castle

Haggis the witch was in a furious temper. She had looked everywhere for her tin-opener. It wasn't surprising that she couldn't find it. Her kitchen was the untidiest, filthiest place you have ever seen. There were piles of dirty plates stacked all over the floor, grimy washing was pegged to huge cobwebs that hung from the ceiling, and the cupboards groaned with her horrible home-made jams and pickles – rats-bane relish, bats-blood chutney and jackal-tooth jam.

'Someone must have taken it!' she cried, kicking over a pile of unwashed cauldrons. 'Oh well, I suppose I'll just have to magic another one!'

Thumbing through an old recipe book, she chanted out all sorts of spells and magic rhymes. Soon the kitchen was full of toys, tin whistles, tiddlywinks and other things beginning with 'T', but she just couldn't get the spell for tin-openers right. She was in a

terrible tantrum.

Then, suddenly, she remembered she'd put it in her hat for safe keeping. Furious, she took it out and set to work on a large tin marked DAMSEL IN DISTRESS.

She went to the door and called, 'Puss, puss, puss!'

There was a distant sound of snuffling and snorting. Soon a small, sleepy, orange dragon shuffled into the kitchen.

'Please stop calling me "Puss",' he grumbled. 'I'm a dragon, and I won't stand for it!'

'I'm sorry, Zoro dear,' Haggis replied. 'But your real name, Zoroaster, is such a mouthful, and we witches are used to having cats to help with spells, not dragons.' In fact she wished sometimes she still had a cat. Dragons were so difficult to feed. 'Come on, eat your din-dins!' she said.

Zoro wondered hopefully if it was his favourite dinner of princess and pickled onions, or even small boy and dumpling stew.

'What d'you think this is?' demanded Haggis, 'a five-star hotel? Now eat up your food like a good boy, and stop being such a fuss-pot!' She tied a napkin under his chin and doled out the contents of the tin on to his plate.

'Oh, not that tinned muck again!' snorted

Zoro crossly. 'No, if I can't have proper princess or real damsel in distress, then I'm going on strike, so there!'

Haggis thought quickly. There weren't many princesses left nowadays, let alone damsels in distress. Goodness only knows, she'd tried hard enough to find one to distress. But if Zoro went on strike, she wouldn't be able to do any magic properly.

Then she remembered reading in her tea leaves the other day about some princess a long way off, who was about to marry a prince something of somewhere else.

'Ah yes,' she mused, 'Princess Polly of Pomerania. Now suppose I pop over to Pomerania on my broomstick – I could have her back here on your plate by tea time tonight!'

'Brilliant idea, Haggis, a positively wizard idea!' said Zoro excitedly. 'Of course, she'd probably need feeding up. In fact I could keep her for my special birthday feast next Tuesday!'

They clasped arms and danced a polka round the kitchen table, with Zoro's tail clattering like sardine cans across the floor.

'Come on then, get your broomstick out!' he panted, falling back against a stack of unwashed crockery, spilling gravy across the

floor.

Haggis took an old broomstick with an outboard motor from a cupboard. She jerked the starter rope, shrieking, 'Forward magic broom!' But though she hissed all sorts of spells and chants, it didn't move an inch.

'Oh well, I'll just have to get the bus, I suppose,' she said. 'I'll catch the number 53 if I hurry! Bye-bye Zoro!'

Just then, the broomstick came to life with a loud bang. As it rose slowly in the air, Haggis leapt astride. With a crash of splintering glass, they flew out of the kitchen window and into the night.

Zoro waved her off and, when she was out of sight, he went to the larder and made himself a huge pickle sandwich.

'Hmmmmm,' he sighed, 'I'm looking forward to a bite of princess again. It's going to be a right royal birthday feast!'

2
Incident at Pomerania Castle

Princess Polly tiptoed out on to the battlements. Good, there was no-one there. Prince Tom had sent her a message, asking her to meet him privately. She leant over the side of a turret and gazed round at the countryside of Pomerania spread out below.

'Where are you?' she called, looking round.

'Here I am!' came the reply, and Prince Tom arrived, looking very puffed and pink after climbing 600 steps in shining armour. He took out a hanky and wiped his brow.

'Why did you ask me to meet you up here?' asked Polly, giving him a kiss.

'Because,' replied Tom, 'I want to give you a love token. Like people did in olden days, you know.'

'What a lovely idea!' Polly exclaimed. 'What is it? I can't wait to see.'

Tom fished around under his shining armour for his pocket, and brought out a little blue bird, which was fast asleep and very crumpled.

'Er, it's a Magic Bird. It was given to me by my godfather, Wizard Idea, when I was a baby,' he said.

'How lovely!' said Polly, smoothing its feathers. 'What sort of magic can it do?'

'Well,' Tom explained, 'it can't actually do magic exactly. It's, er, supposed to give one good advice in times of trouble. I've never needed it so far, luckily.'

'I must give you a token, too,' said Polly. 'Look after my lovely Magic Bird for a moment. I'll just run down to my room to see what I can find.'

Prince Tom took off his helmet and brought out some fruit cake he'd been keeping under there since breakfast. He scattered some crumbs on the ground for the Magic Bird, then he leant over the edge of the battlements, his long fair hair streaming forward like a banner.

Haggis was cruising low over Pomerania on her broomstick, looking for Pomerania Castle, Polly's home. In front of her was a guide book of the castle, spread out on the handle of the broomstick.

She snapped the guide book shut. How on earth was she going to get into the castle, let alone find Princess Polly, let alone get her out again unnoticed, even in the large black bag she'd brought specially.

Then her eyes lighted on the turrets of Pomerania far below.

'Oh well,' she said, 'I might as well have a quick whirl round it and see what I can see.' And she dropped several hundred feet and started circling round the castle.

Imagine her surprise when, through her binoculars, she saw Prince Tom leaning over the battlements, throwing pieces of cake to the crocodiles in the moat far below.

'Why, that must be Princess Polly herself!' Haggis exclaimed. 'You can always tell a princess by her long golden hair. What a stroke of luck, her being out here just waiting for me!'

Like a hawk from the sky, she dropped down on Prince Tom and popped her black bag over his head. Grabbing him by his feet, she took off again on her broomstick.

Prince Tom's muffled cries of, 'I say, this is jolly beastly!' and, 'This definitely isn't cricket!' were lost in the wind, as Haggis, broomstick and black bag hurtled through the gathering gloom.

Princess Polly came puffing up the spiral staircase again, just in time to see Haggis

disappearing. She called Prince Tom, but there was no answer. She rushed to the edge of the battlements, afraid he might have fallen over.

'You won't find him there!' said a perky voice. It was the Magic Bird that Tom had given her. 'Tom's been kidnapped by Haggis, a wicked witch!'

Now, Polly knew that this sort of thing only happened in fairy stories, and at first she didn't believe the bird. But he promised her it was true.

Polly paced up and down a while. What on earth was she to do?

'Well,' she said at last to the bird, 'you're supposed to be magic so give me some good advice.'

The bird coughed. 'I always do this sort of thing in poetry,' he explained.

> 'Far in Northern lands now go,
> To Wizard Idea in his land of snow.
> He alone has power to quell
> The magic hold of Haggis' spell.
> Travel through one day and night,
> To the North Pole, then turn right.'

'Good heavens!' said Polly. 'So you really do give advice in times of trouble. Now what was it? Go and see Wizard Idea. He's Tom's

godfather, and he lives miles away. We must leave immediately. Prince Tom must be rescued!'

She rushed downstairs and packed a few things into a red-spotted hanky. She hurried to the royal stables and leapt on to the finest racehorse. Then she galloped over the drawbridge and on over the countryside beyond.

She left a note on her dressing table saying: Please cancel all royal engagements (including wedding) until further notice.

3
Wizard Idea

All day Polly travelled northwards, and towards evening she reached the Northern lands. There she changed the tired racehorse for a sledge pulled by eight polar bears. Wrapping herself in her father's coronation robes, which she had thoughtfully taken to keep her warm, she sped on through the snow dunes under the frosty stars.

At last, just before dawn, she reached the North Pole, a shimmering needle of ice dazzling in the grey light. There she turned right, and as she did so, the sun mounted the horizon and she saw the pinnacles of a castle far away in the golden-pink light of dawn.

'This must be Wizard Idea's castle!' she said.

It was a tiny little castle when you came up close. Everything was neat and freshly painted and, in spite of the snow, there were window-boxes full of bright flowers at every window.

19

She pulled the bell-rope outside the front door. Out shot a little wooden bird like in a cuckoo clock, then the door opened and she went in. A little, shrivelled old wizard was hobbling across the hall. His cheeks were pink as raspberries, and his nose was as purple and shiny as an aubergine. His hair was white and frizzy and stood up on end.

'Ah ha!' he beamed welcomingly. 'It's Princess Polly. I knew you'd come and see me one day. How d'you do. I knew your mother ... or was it your grandmother ...? I can't remember. Time flies so quickly when you're a wizard, you see.'

Polly quickly told him that his godson, Tom, had been kidnapped, and that the Magic Bird he'd given Tom a long time ago had advised her to come straight to him, as he was the only person who had any power against Haggis the witch.

The old wizard listened through an ear trumpet to her story, but when he heard Haggis' name, he stopped her.

'Haggis the witch, eh? My old enemy Haggis. Oh dear, to be perfectly honest, my dear, there's nothing much I can do. You see, a long time ago, Haggis stole my magic staff. She did it just to spite me and to stop me interfering in her evil plans, because it's no

use to her otherwise. Without my staff, I can't do any decent magic, just a few party tricks.' At this, a goldfish suddenly swam out of his pocket and disappeared with a pop.

'Can't you get your staff back, if it's so important?' Polly asked impatiently.

'No good,' sighed the wizard. 'Haggis broke it into three pieces and gave them all away. She knew I wouldn't be able to travel about all over the world looking for them, not with my rheumatism.'

Polly thought for a moment. 'I don't suppose if we just left Prince Tom to it, he could rescue himself?'

'No chance,' replied the wizard. 'Haggis probably kidnapped him to feed her pet dragon, Zoroaster. Talking of dragons, was it your mother or grandmother who got eaten by that purple dragon . . . dreadful business!'

But Polly wasn't listening. She'd had a sudden brilliant idea.

Seizing the wizard in a grasp that made him wince, she cried, 'I know, I'll go and get the three pieces of the magic staff back myself!'

'Brilliant idea, my dear, brilliant!' he replied, nursing his hand. 'But the task will be long and dangerous. Are you sure you'll be up to it?'

'Just tell me what to do and let me try!' said Polly.

So Wizard Idea told Polly that Haggis had given the first piece of staff to an ogre, called Sheamus O'Gre. He lived in a castle in the West, and used the piece of staff as the handle of his ogre's club.

The second piece of staff had been given to a terrible sorceress named the Cuppandsorceress. She used it as a magic spoon for stirring potions to turn people into statues.

'And her address?' asked Polly, who was

writing all this down in a notebook. It seemed the address was simply, Cuppandsorceress Castle, the East.

'The third piece,' said the wizard, 'might be the most difficult to find. It was given to Bloggs, the clown, from Pandora's Magic Circus. They travel all over the world doing shows. I don't know where you'll find them. Pity, I used to love clowns,' and he absent-mindedly produced a flower from the top of his hat, which squirted Polly with water. He chortled feebly.

'Now do be careful of the ogre and the sorceress, my dear,' he added, becoming serious again. 'Even wizards are wary of such creatures.'

'Don't worry,' said Polly gaily. 'I can look after myself. I'll be back with the three pieces of your magic staff as soon as possible. There's no time to lose if we're going to rescue poor Tom in time.'

And with that she was off, leaving Wizard Idea tut-tutting anxiously after her.

4

Sheamus O'Gre

Polly rushed out of Wizard Idea's castle, jumped back into the sledge, and cracked a huge whip over the polar bears' heads. They leapt into a lolloping gallop and the snow flurried up on all sides as they sped away.

The Magic Bird, who'd been fast asleep inside Polly's cloak, suddenly woke up.

'Where are we off to now?' he asked sleepily.

'To the West to see Sheamus O'Gre,' Polly explained.

'I suppose you did ask the wizard how to get there, didn't you?' asked the Magic Bird.

'Oh no! I forgot!' shouted Polly. 'We'll have to go back.' She reined in the bears so suddenly that they skidded, collided and landed in a heap. She got out of the sledge and helped them back on to their paws.

'I'm sorry, bears, but we'll have to go back to Wizard Idea's castle. I've no idea how to actually get to the West. I just knew we had to get there quickly.'

The Magic Bird fluttered out of her cloak and hopped on to the seat of the sledge.

'You headstrong, headlong girl!' he scolded. 'If you're going to do adventures properly, you must think and plan, THINK and PLAN, yes! Otherwise you'll just get us all into a mess. However, it's lucky you have a Magic Bird with you who knows a thing or two about adventures.'

'I don't suppose you know how to get to the West?' asked Polly.

'Magic Birds don't give you all the answers. We only give clues to help you help yourself. Now listen, if we leave the North Star at our backs, and travel back the way we came for a day and a night, we shall come to the Great Signpost in the middle of the world. Then you'll see what to do.'

The sledge started up again, and they sped on mile after mile through the frosty wasteland. At last they passed out of the land of snow and, at the frontier, she found her father's racehorse waiting, rested and refreshed, to take her on the next stage of her journey.

Sadly she said goodbye to the bears, mounted the horse and galloped onwards. Soon they reached the Great Signpost in the middle of the world. It pointed in four directions: North, East, South and West. Polly turned right towards the West.

A seemingly endless stony road led them through barren landscapes of rocks and cacti. After riding all night and all day, they saw in the distance the craggy mountain ranges of the West, beyond which lay the shore at the end of the world. Their journey through the mountains was long and difficult, but they passed through them at last, and came to that vast shore.

Far off on the horizon, beyond the mighty sweep of white sands along the coastline, Polly could just see the outline of a great castle. She galloped along the beach and up the steep mound to the castle gate. Outside was a notice.

O'GRE'S CASTLE. NATIONAL TRUST PROPERTY OF GREAT HISTORICAL IMPORTANCE. VISITORS 70p. CHILDREN 30p.

Princess Polly was just searching for some money, when a great voice boomed from the battlements.

'Who goes there?'

'No-one in particular,' piped Polly nervously. 'Just a tourist come to visit your castle. It is open to the public, isn't it?'

'It certainly is. The public is always

O'GRE'S CASTLE

NATIONAL TRUST
PROPERTY OF GREAT
NATIONAL IMPORTANCE

VISITORS 7Op
CHILDREN 3Op
O'GRES IN ARMS
FREE

RING

welcome to my castle!' said the voice. 'Hang on and I'll come down and let you in.'

There was a clatter of hobnail boots on stone stairs, and a gruff muttering which sounded like, 'Oh I wish I hadn't eaten the footman!' Then the gate suddenly opened.

There stood a grey greenish ogre with long pointed ears on the side of his head, and two or three teeth jutting out of his grin.

'Sheamus O'Gre at your service. And this here be O'Gre's Castle. Now, let me show you round, young lady.'

'That's very kind of you,' said Princess Polly, making a special note of the ogre's club sticking out of his belt. 'It's a magnificent castle. Do you live here all alone?' she asked nervously, anxious to keep him talking, so that she could quickly think of a plan.

Sheamus explained that he used to live there with his brother Paddy. But Paddy had been slain by a knight in shining armour. He was dreadfully lonely now. Visitors came, but they never seemed to stay long. (At this he kicked a skull out of his path.) Most of all, he missed all the wonderful games that he and Paddy used to play.

Polly was amazed to hear that ogres actually played games, but Sheamus assured her that ogres were only human, and liked a bit of fun. They used to play leap-frog, I spy, Ogre Grady says, and many others. But his favourite game of all had been Blind Ogre's Buff.

'I see,' said Polly. She was already thinking of a scheme to get the ogre's club off him. Perhaps she could persuade him to play Blind Ogre's Buff, then run off with the club while he was blindfolded. But oh dear, suppose she mistimed it! Suppose she had to wrestle with him! Suppose there was a fight to the death! It was too dreadful to think about. But there was nothing else to do! It was too late to turn back now.

Meanwhile, Sheamus was chewing over the possibility of eating Polly. He'd eaten a whole coach-load of tourists that week, but they were pensioners, and rather tough, even when cooked for hours in an Irish stew. Now Polly was a pretty piece of flesh, and would only need lightly frying in butter.

'... and mushrooms,' he added aloud.

'I beg your pardon?' asked Polly.

'Mushrooms ... much room, I mean there's too much room here for one ogre. I'm terribly lonely,' Sheamus quickly returned.

So Polly suggested that they could play one of the games now. Sheamus jumped up and down in excitement. A game would just work

up a good appetite for tea, he thought. He could enjoy a few rounds of Blind Ogre's Buff, then while Polly was blindfolded, give her a quick bonk with his club, and stick her straight in a pan. He took off the scarf his granny had knitted him and started tying it over Polly's eyes.

But Polly cleverly pretended that she'd never played the game before, and needed to see how it was done first. Sheamus agreed, and they tied the scarf tightly round his head, so that he could see nothing.

'Now we must turn you round,' said Polly.

She turned the ogre round and round until he complained he was giddy.

'And now I'm going to catch you!' said the ogre. He blundered this way and that, trying to grab Polly, stumbling over bones and pieces of fallen masonry. But she darted away, leading him a proper dance round the castle, up winding stairways, along battlements, and in and out of dark passageways.

'That's right, tire him out, then grab his ogre's club!' squawked the Magic Bird, excitedly jumping around on Polly's shoulder.

'Speak up, and don't talk in silly voices!' Sheamus called. 'Where are you? Give me a clue.' He lumbered blindly past Polly with hands outstretched.

Quick as a flash, Polly crept up behind him and seized the ogre's club.

Sheamus snatched out and grabbed Polly by the hood of her cloak.

'Give me back that club, or I'll eat you!' he roared.

'Oh no you don't! It's bad manners to eat your visitors!' replied Polly, and she swung the club up in the air and crashed it down on Sheamus' bald head. 'Take that, you horrible ogre!'

Sheamus fell to the ground, pulling her down with him. He lashed about horribly with his thin hairy arms and his knobbly knees, crushing her beneath him. The ogre's club spun through the air and landed just out of her reach. She fought and kicked madly. She must get that ogre's club at all costs!

The Magic Bird fluttered this way and that above their heads as they struggled.

'Come on, Polly! Come on, Polly!' he squawked. 'Try to distract his attention! Play another game!'

Polly thought quickly as Sheamus' hands

tightened round her throat.

'Ogre Grady ... um, Ogre Grady says, put your hands on your head!' she shouted desperately.

To her surprise, Sheamus sat up immediately and put his hands on his head. Polly seized her opportunity. She also seized the ogre's club.

'Ogre Grady says, take that! Ogre Grady says, fall down flat on your nose!' she commanded, as she brought the club down twice more on Sheamus' head.

'Ogre ... gracious!' wailed Sheamus. 'I'm seeing stars ... it must be heaven!' And he flopped forward, and lay senseless at her feet. Several green stars floated upwards from his ears.

'Oh dear,' said Polly. 'I didn't really mean to hit him quite that hard. Still, he was going to eat me, and I have got the first piece of Wizard Idea's magic staff now. I mustn't waste time crying over spilt ... ogres. I must set off immediately for the East!'

She stepped quickly over Sheamus' body. He was only dazed, but luckily for Polly, he suffered from loss of memory, and could later remember nothing of the incident. In fact, he spent several weeks looking for his ogre's club.

5

Journey to the East

When they got outside the castle, Polly was tired out and longed for a rest, but the Magic Bird pointed out that Sheamus might wake up at any minute and chase them. There was no sign of the racehorse. He had obviously bolted at the first sight of the ogre. There was nothing for it but to walk.

Polly trudged on along the coast for several hours, till she came to another signpost. This one pointed in one direction only. It said: TO THE EAST – LONG WAY; but above that a small arrow pointed up at an angle, and written on it were the words: EAST – SHORT CUT. WET WEATHER ONLY.

Polly was just wondering whether it would be quicker to wait for rain, or to set off immediately the long way, when a shrill voice said, 'Wait for rain. There'll be some soon. I can feel it in my feathers. They work like seaweed, you see.'

It was the Magic Bird, of course. He'd been

fast asleep inside her cloak. Polly wasn't sure she wanted to listen to his good advice any more. She was beginning to wish she'd just sent the Royal Artillery along after Haggis to rescue Prince Tom in the first place.

However, she lay down on the ground and said, 'All right then, wake me up when it's raining.' She wasn't bad-tempered really, but she was very tired, and rather shaken by the Sheamus O'Gre incident.

She was woken up about two hours later by raindrops falling on her face.

'Wake up!' said the Magic Bird. 'Look!'

She jumped up quickly, and there, stretching into the distant horizon, was a huge rainbow, with brass bannisters. It seemed hazy, as though you would put your foot straight through, but no, it was firm, almost bouncy. You could run up it two steps at a time with ease.

Now she saw the point of waiting for the rain.

'Come on, Magic Bird!' she cried. 'We're off to the East!'

The bird skimmed ahead of her through the rainbow mists. It was the most beautiful thing she had ever seen. How wonderful it would be, she thought, to slide down the bannisters on the other side! She was half-running, half-floating up into the clouds. She stopped to look over the side at the tiny towns and villages far below. Then they went on up through the cloud line, where it suddenly became foggy and dark. She groped for the rail, faltering.

'This way, this way!' called the Magic Bird, just above her head.

Suddenly they came through the fog and gazed out on an enormous continent of cloud below them.

'No time to admire the view,' said the bird. 'The sun's setting, and we don't want to be lost in the night sky.'

And so Polly ran on and on, right over the top of the rainbow.

'We're starting the descent now,' said the Magic Bird.

Suddenly Polly felt her knees collapse beneath her. She was sliding down a giant slide which reached from the sky, down through the clouds, to, she hoped, the earth below. The rainbow mists seemed to swirl and spiral through her as she sped down. It was like whizzing through a giant kaleidoscope.

Down she went till she saw the earth zooming towards her: vast stretches of sea and desert. Suddenly she realised she had shot

right off the end of the rainbow, and was turning over and over in space like a diver. Then it was all over, and she landed with a soft thud in a sand dune.

Polly got up slowly, and gazed around her. There was sand everywhere. But there, towards the East, she saw something shining. She could just make out through the heat haze a small palace with onion-shaped domes.

As she approached, she could see the palace was surrounded by a beautiful garden with cedar trees and exotic flowers. Peacocks strutted down avenues, and panthers lay idly washing themselves in the shade. Little fountains here and there sent up delicate fans of water spray. Everything looked tempting and cool to a weary desert traveller.

'I'm sure this must be the Cuppandsorceress' palace,' said the Magic Bird. 'Come on, let's go and explore.'

But as they reached the great iron gates Polly saw that four huge tigers lay guarding the entrance to the oasis paradise. They sat up with hackles raised when they saw her, and growled in chorus. She stood still, afraid to move. The tigers edged slowly forwards, waving their cruel paws at her. She wanted to panic. The Magic Bird fluttered out of reach –

if only she could fly out of reach too! The
tigers moved nearer, and crouched, ready to
pounce.

'I must throw something!' she thought. But
what? There were pebbles at her feet, but if
she bent down, the tigers would be on her in a
flash. She edged backwards, feeling in her
pockets. A box of drawing pins, a little pot
of glue and some string, all for emergencies,
and . . . oh yes, a ham sandwich.

Quick as lightning, she took the sandwich
and flung it back over her shoulder. The
tigers bounded furiously after it and started
fighting for the delicious morsel. Polly didn't

wait to watch. She ran in through the gates and crashed them shut, leaving the tigers tearing each other limb from limb outside.

'You handled that very well,' said the Magic Bird, fluttering back down on to her shoulder. 'Thanks to my good advice, you're really becoming pretty good at adventures.'

Polly started to laugh, but her laughter soon froze when several black panthers bounded over and circled her. 'Oh no!' she thought. 'Out of the frying pan into the fire!'

She pretended not to be scared. 'Down boys, down!' she commanded and, to her great surprise, instead of snarling at her, the panthers sat down obediently.

'Why, they must be tame!' she said to the Magic Bird.

'Maybe they are victims of the Cuppand-sorceress' magic,' said the Bird. 'People that she's turned into creatures to be living ornaments in her garden.'

'Perhaps so,' replied Polly, stroking the panthers. They rubbed themselves against her, purring blissfully like huge cats. 'Oh dear, I'd love to stay stroking you all day, but I've got a prince to rescue, and time's getting short.'

She walked through the garden to the palace, with the Magic Bird fluttering behind her. What a beautiful palace it was! The domes were covered with beaten gold, and the sides were decorated with sky-blue mosaics. The arches over the windows were encrusted with jewels that glinted like tigers' eyes. A heavy, sleepy magic seemed to breathe through the very walls.

6
The Cuppandsorceress

The Magic Bird suggested they should split up to find the best way to get in. So he flew up through an upper window to explore, while Polly crept round the back of the palace. She peered in through each arched window as she went. There was no sign of anyone anywhere.

One window had a stone lattice-work pattern over the front. She put her eyes over one of the holes and looked in. It was dark inside, with speckles of sunlight thrown by the patterns on the window. She could just make out statues of men, women and children silently waiting in the cool hush of a museum.

Suddenly the door at the far end swung open with a crash, and a slinky lady dressed in shimmering green swept in. On her head was a helmet with horns on either side, over which she had curled her long, dark tresses. She was bewitchingly beautiful, but every inch an enchantress. Polly shuddered. This must indeed be the Cuppandsorceress!

The sorceress had a feather duster, and she began lightly dusting each statue in turn.

'Good morning, darlings,' she said in a husky voice. 'How are you today, my pretty ones? I must have you in good shape for my great exhibition next week. The only exhibition in which all the visitors will end up as exhibits!' She laughed out loud, and the sound echoed through the museum. But the statues remained dumb.

The Cuppandsorceress chuckled again, and tossed the duster up into the air. With a flash, it turned into a long spoon. The sorceress caught it and swept out through the door.

Polly realised immediately that the spoon was in fact the second piece of Wizard Idea's magic staff. Somehow or other, she must get into the palace and steal the spoon, or trick the sorceress into giving it to her.

She went on walking round, looking for a way in. Suddenly she heard a shrill squawk from inside, followed by another burst of cruel laughter.

'The Magic Bird!' thought Polly, and rushed in the direction of the sound. It came from an upper window. She would have to climb up the creeper that covered that part of the wall. It had a sturdy enough stem, but it

45

was laden with scented flowers which had attracted swarms of huge bees.

Polly didn't like the look of those fierce, tiger-striped, fat-bellied bees one bit. But if the Magic Bird was in trouble . . . well! So she started climbing.

The bees buzzed angrily round her as she hauled herself up through the blossoms. They stung her hands and swarmed round her face. She felt giddy from the scent of the flowers and the poison of the bee stings. But she managed to heave herself on to the ledge of the window and peer in.

There was a beautiful carved bed in one

corner, and ... oh no! Hanging from the ceiling was an ornate birdcage, and inside was a statue of a dear little bird. It was the Magic Bird! Not fluffy and brightly feathered any more, but frozen to white marble. Beneath the swinging cage several feathers fluttered sadly.

'Magic Bird!' she murmured in despair. The world turned slowly on its axis; she fell back through the creepers and remembered nothing more.

When Polly came round, she was inside the palace. She was lying on a soft pile of cushions in a richly decorated room. Great folds of golden drapery hung all around, from ceiling to floor.

She heard a sound behind her and quickly shut her eyes.

'What a delightful statue she'll make – just right for my collection!' said a voice. It was the Cuppandsorceress.

She came and sat down beside Polly and brushed her long fingers soothingly over Polly's brow. Polly looked up, and found herself gazing into two eyes as deep and dangerous as pools of piranha fish.

'Hello, darling!' purred the sorceress. 'You had a teensy-weensy little accident. But you have nothing to fear! I found you and looked after you. You're safe with me!'

'You must be the terrible ... the terribly beautiful ... Cuppandsorceress!' Polly faltered.

'That's right, darling, but you may call me Cuppa! But who are you, and what brings you across the desert to my palace?'

'My name is Princess Polly, and I'm on a quest to rescue a knight in shining armour from a dragon.'

'A dragon! How frightfully brave of you. But do be careful, darling, dragons can be dreadfully dangerous, and we don't want that lovely complexion scratched, do we?' She rose and slunk across to a table on which there were various bottles of colourful liquids. 'However, to refresh you after your long and tiring adventures, I'll mix you a Cuppandsorceress Special.'

Polly saw her mix several liquids in a goblet, and thought she heard the words:

> *'Ashes to ashes, skin and bone*
> *Turn the princess into stone!'*

The sorceress stirred the steaming potion with her long spoon and came across to Polly, humming softly. Polly quickly shut her eyes and pretended to have dozed off.

48

'Wake up, darling. You must drink something first, and then you can sleep. You can sleep as long as you like!' She laughed softly.

'Like my Magic Bird!' said Polly. 'You made him go to sleep all right!'

'Ah! So it was *your* Magic Bird, was it? You sent him snooping about inside my palace, did you?' the sorceress hissed. But then she suddenly became all kindness again. 'I'm sorry, darling. It's just that one can't be too careful nowadays. I have a certain valuable possession that spies are out to find. You shall have your Magic Bird back, of course, but first, drink up this potion ... I mean, refreshing drink.' She put the goblet to Polly's lips.

Polly jumped up and, seizing the sorceress by her hair, so that her helmet crashed to the floor, she snatched the steaming goblet and emptied it into the sorceress' mouth.

'Drink it yourself!' she cried. The sorceress gulped and spluttered and shrieked, but in her surprise she swallowed the potion.

'Darling!' she choked. 'You have ruined me! AAAGH! I'm turning ... into ... a statue!' These last words came out slowly, as she was indeed turning to stone.

'You make a wonderful statue!' said Polly, wrenching the spoon from the sorceress' marble clutches, and putting it in her pocket with the first piece of Wizard Idea's staff. 'But now I've got the spoon, I must rescue the poor Magic Bird!'

She rushed up the wide staircase and searched in all the upper rooms, till she came to the one with the bird-cage. She could hardly believe her eyes. The Magic Bird was fluttering about inside, as fluffy and feathery as ever.

'What kept you so long?' he chirped. 'I had to take on the Cuppandsorceress single-handed!' He explained how the sorceress had hit him on the beak with her long spoon and he had suddenly gone cold all over.

Polly realised that, when the Cuppandsorceress had swallowed her own magic, it must have suddenly undone all the evil spells she'd cast on her victims. She told the bird exactly what had happened, and showed him the spoon.

The Magic Bird was very pleased with her. 'You've done very well. In fact, you're almost getting to the stage where you don't need advice any more! However, there is still one more task ahead. We must find Pandora's Magic Circus, and Bloggs the clown, without delay. Goodness only knows what has happened to Prince Tom by now!'

'But where do we even begin to look for

them?' said Polly, despairingly. 'Wizard Idea said they travel all over the world. I'm fed up with all this rushing around having adventures. I just want to sleep.' This last task suddenly seemed the hardest one of all.

She sat down on the huge bed. 'Oh wouldn't it be lovely to lie down and have a little nap, Magic Bird? Couldn't we, please?'

So Polly curled up on the bed and the Magic Bird nestled up against her with his head tucked under his wing, and they both fell fast asleep. Polly dreamt of huge ogres chasing her over endless deserts, of witches throwing her into bottomless cauldrons, and dragons crunching up whole armies of knights in shining armour. The Magic Bird dreamt of his comfortable perch in Wizard Idea's castle, and bird seed, and bird baths, and birds' nests.

7

The Twizzle Stick

Neither Polly nor the Magic Bird heard all the rumpus that was going on downstairs. They slept right through all the noise of shouting, cheering, and celebration, and never stirred.

You see, just as the Magic Bird was set free when the Cuppandsorceress drank her own poison, so all the other statues had unfrozen and come to life. Slowly they blinked, stretched and yawned, as if waking up after a long, long sleep.

Crowds of people emerged from all over the palace, and gathered in the garden, laughing, singing and hugging each other. Some rushed about, collecting baggage or leading animals and wagons out of the sorceress' stables – elephants, plumed horses, bears, panthers, dogs, even camels. There were men with giant shoes and funny hats, ladies in glittering tutus, acrobats, stilt walkers, fire eaters, trapeze artists, jesters and all sorts of others.

Of course you must have guessed by now. The Cuppandsorceress had turned a whole circus into statues. She had locked away all the animals, except the panthers, whom she kept as ornamental pets for her garden. How long they had all been under her spell, none of them knew, but they decided to set off immediately, and follow the road wherever it took them.

The circus band struck up a gay tune, and a line of painted caravans full of people and animals streamed out through the gates, past four snarling stone tigers, and on, and on, and on along the road.

It wasn't till the next day that Polly woke up. The Magic Bird was pecking her.

'Wake up, Polly, there's not a moment to lose!' he fretted.

Polly jumped out of bed.

'Good heavens!' she cried. 'How could I sleep at a time like this! Poor Prince Tom! Haggis has probably boiled him up and served him to that dragon with mashed potatoes by now!'

'Or roasted him and served him up with redcurrant jelly,' added the Bird gloomily.

'Or pickled him and served him up with gherkins!' wailed Polly. 'We must start searching for Bloggs the clown immediately.'

The Magic Bird reckoned the only thing to do was to ask anyone they saw if they'd heard of Pandora's Magic Circus. They noticed signs that a great number of animals and people had been trampling through the garden. But the place was deserted; there was no-one around to tell them what had happened.

The road from the palace led on across the desert. Polly trudged wearily mile after mile, till at last, towards evening, they came to a little village. Polly rested at an inn, where she was told that a circus had passed that way only the day before. Unfortunately, no-one could remember what it was called, or which road it had taken out of the village.

'I must catch them up and find out who they are,' Polly told the Bird. 'Wouldn't it be incredible if it was actually Pandora's Magic Circus!'

Beyond the village, the road forked in two directions, though the shifting sands made it difficult to make out any road at all. Desert winds had wiped out any tracks the circus might have left. The signpost was no help either. It just pointed NORTH-EAST in one direction, and SOUTH-EAST in the other.

'But look at this!' said the Magic Bird. At

56

the base of the signpost, someone had stuck a poster. It read: PANDORA'S MAGIC CIRCUS. GRAND SHOW TONIGHT. ENTRY FREE.

'I can't believe it! So it really is them! Our troubles are nearly over!' Polly cried.

'There's just one problem,' said the Bird. 'We still don't know which way to go, because they don't say where the show is to be held.'

'Oh no! You're right!' said Polly. 'I suppose we'll just have to guess, and risk getting it wrong. We might lose them altogether!'

'We must make up our minds quickly,' said the Bird. 'I can feel the wind in my feathers.

I wouldn't be surprised if there wasn't a sandstorm blowing up.'

In the end he settled it by doing Eeny, Meeny, Miney, Mo. It came out at North-East. There was nothing for it but to set off and just hope they found the circus.

The desert wind was getting stronger every minute. Sand whipped round them, and the dunes heaved and shifted like great waves before their eyes. The road became impossible to follow. Polly, wrapped in her cloak with the Magic Bird safe inside, was buffeted this way and that, blinded by whiplashes of sand.

Further and further off course, she stumbled in the raging sandstorm, half-running, half-crawling. Flying objects spiralled across her path.

Suddenly she was flung against a hard surface. Then she heard voices. Hands came out and pulled her to safety. She was in some kind of shelter. She could breathe again. She was safe.

Polly found herself inside a painted caravan. The sandstorm was howling outside, but in here it was safe and cosy. There was a delicious smell of fresh scones and tea. The Magic Bird hopped out of her cloak and looked around.

'Got lost in the sandstorm, eh?' said a voice. She turned round and saw a funny person with a red nose and a stripy hat – a clown!

'Oh yes,' said Polly, 'it was dreadful. I couldn't see a thing! I must have been blown miles off course. Thank you so much for pulling me to safety.'

'Well, I heard a terrific clonk on the side of the caravan. I didn't know what it could be. Then I saw it was a person, so I brought you inside. Of course I can see you're not one of us circus people,' he said, pouring her a cup of tea.

'No,' said Polly, 'but I am looking for a circus. I don't suppose you could help me, being in the same line of business?' She explained how she had seen the poster for Pandora's Magic Circus on the signpost, and was hoping to find it.

'You need look no further, lady. This is Pandora's Magic Circus! We were just setting up for the show, when this sandstorm came whizzing along, whisking up the Big Top, tent poles and all. Goodness only knows where everyone has got to, or what's happened to all the animals!'

'That's marvellous!' cried Polly. 'I mean it's marvellous that I've found Pandora's Circus, but terrible about the sandstorm. Actually, it's Bloggs the clown I'm looking for. Do you know him?'

'Know him? I'd have a job not knowing him! I'm Bloggs the clown. Now, how can I help?'

Polly recounted the whole story. How Haggis had kidnapped poor Prince Tom to feed her dragon, how the Magic Bird had sent her to Wizard Idea, the adventure with Sheamus O'Gre, and all about the Cuppandsorceress' spoon.

'The Cuppandsorceress, eh? I know all about her!' said Bloggs. 'Now listen, I think I know just what you need.' He went to a drawer beneath the high bed at the end of the caravan, and took out a brightly coloured wand with feathers at the end.

'What's that?' asked Polly.

'It's a twizzle stick. Most clowns have them,' said Bloggs.

'Twizzle stick – of course! The third piece of Wizard Idea's staff!' chirped the Magic Bird excitedly. Until now he had kept silent.

'Well, I always knew there was something special about it!' said Bloggs. 'Take it, dear lady, it's yours. We don't need magic in the circus. The circus has its own kind of magic.'

Bloggs went on to explain how, years before, he'd been given the twizzle stick by an old lady on the road. Polly guessed at once that the old lady had been Haggis. Somehow or other the Cuppandsorceress had got to know about it, and had invited the whole circus to her palace to perform. But Bloggs had refused to give her the twizzle stick; he had hidden it down his sock. In her rage she had turned every one of them into statues. There they had remained, frozen in her museum, until two days ago, when they had suddenly found themselves free.

By this time the storm had died down. Bloggs opened the door of the caravan and they looked out. What a scene met their eyes! Everywhere there were bits of circus covered with sand. The circus people were beginning to emerge. Some were digging out their caravans, others were hauling on half-buried ropes. Polly and Bloggs joined in the rescue operation. Within a few hours, all the missing people and animals had been found and the Big Top had been erected, ready for the show that night.

Polly wished she could stay and watch the show – she loved circuses. Everything looked so exciting and the people were so friendly.

'Tell you what, we'll come and do a special show at your wedding feast!' said Bloggs, and he added with an embarrassed cough, 'That is, if we rescue Prince Tom in time.'

But how was Polly to get the three pieces of Wizard Idea's staff back in time to save Tom? The rainbow staircase only went in one direction, and it was far too far from East to North to travel overland.

'Well, I have got one idea,' said Bloggs. 'But it might be dangerous.'

He led Polly through the striped tents and caravans, into the Big Top itself. There, on one side of the arena, a huge cannon was being polished.

'How do you fancy being a human cannon-ball? This cannon would shoot you back to the North Pole in no time!' he said.

Polly didn't fancy the idea one little bit, but she knew it would save a lot of precious time. So Bloggs took her to meet Tyrone Tuggit, the circus strong man and Master of the Human Cannon.

Tyrone was delighted to have a volunteer who was actually willing to be shot all the way to the North Pole. But he insisted that Polly must wait till the Big Show that night. Then she could be the star attraction, and thousands of people could see her daring feat.

Polly reluctantly agreed, though the Magic Bird was not at all happy. Princess Polly was turning out to be a great deal too adventurous for his liking. He much preferred giving advice to nice, quiet, slightly timid people.

So Polly was kitted out with a special sparkling acrobat's outfit, which had a pouch for the Magic Bird to travel in. People had begun to arrive from all the surrounding desert villages and soon the show began.

First there was a grand parade round the arena while the band played. Polly was allowed to sit on one of the elephants. She suddenly felt very excited when she heard all the children shouting, the gay circus music and the carnival atmosphere. She almost forgot to feel nervous.

After the parade she sat and watched the trapeze artists do their high wire act. Then came the lions and panthers, pretending to be very fierce while their trainer made them do tricks. (Polly, of course, knew they were quite tame.) After that there were the plumed ponies, performing seals, the tightrope walkers – and the clowns.

Bloggs drove into the arena in a battered old fire engine that suddenly went up in smoke. All the other clowns rushed in to help him fix it, and somehow or other they all got soaked with water and foam and custard pies. Polly laughed till tears ran down her cheeks.

Then suddenly she heard the Ringmaster announce, 'Ladies and gentlemen, boys and girls! You are about to see the highlight of the whole evening! Princess Polly of Pomerania has volunteered to become a human cannonball!' Gasps of amazement could be heard all round. 'Princess Polly will enter the Human Cannon, and will be shot, ladies and gentlemen, all the way to the North Pole!'

There was a tremendous burst of applause and stamping of feet from the audience.

No-one had ever heard of such a daring feat being performed before. Polly felt sick, but somehow she managed to walk to the centre of the arena. She gave a small wave to the crowds, hoping they wouldn't notice her knees quaking and her teeth rattling.

Then, just as she was trying to think of an excuse to back down, Bloggs the clown appeared at her side, and announced to the audience that he was going with her. He gave her hand a quick squeeze.

'You're going to need a bit of help with Haggis and that dragon, I reckon!' he whispered.

So it was decided. Together, they fixed parachutes to their backs and climbed the ladder up into the Human Cannon. Then down, down into the dark inside they went. Everyone cheered madly when Tyrone Tuggit lit the fuse.

There was a long pause, and then a BANG! Polly felt herself hurtling through space in an explosion of colours and stars. Up and up they were flung by a great force, till they could see the North Star as close above them as a hot air balloon. Still clinging tightly together, they heard soft fluttering noises above them, as the rainbow-coloured parachutes opened out. The parachutes slowed down their upward surge, and for some moments they seemed to hang suspended in space. Then down, down they floated through unknown grey worlds of shadows.

Polly held on tightly to Bloggs as they floated on down. Soon, beneath them, they could see the snowy mountains of the North, with their beautiful ice canyons. They drifted through frozen crags, swooping and gliding like huge birds over bottomless valleys.

Then icy air currents caught them up, and carried them at terrifying speed, mile upon mile, across frozen wastelands. But at last, a sudden squall brought them down to earth, right in the middle of Wizard Idea's back garden – where they got hopelessly tangled up in his washing line!

8
Wizard Idea Again

'Shoo, shoo!' called a shaky voice from the kitchen window. It was Wizard Idea himself. He came hobbling out with a long-handled broom, and started poking the crumpled parachutes.

'Ow!' said Polly, scrabbling wildly to free herself from the folds of the material. Wizard

Idea nearly jumped out of his skin when Polly crawled out.

'Good heavens!' he exclaimed. 'If it isn't dear Princess Polly! Back again so soon? I wasn't expecting you for ages, perhaps ... never!'

'Yes, Wizard, it's really me. The Magic Bird's here as well, safe and sound. Now, there's no time to lose. I've got all three pieces of your magic staff. We must stick them together again quickly, so we can rescue Prince Tom!'

'What's that, my dear? You've got the three pieces? Well done, well done! Now in my day, it was the boys who rescued the girls. Why I remember when I was a mere slip of a wizard ...'

But suddenly Bloggs rose up from the pile of parachutes, making the old wizard jump again. Bloggs introduced himself with a bow, and explained how he and Polly had travelled back from the East. The wizard was extremely interested in the Human Cannon as a form of transport. He himself, he explained, was working on a new invention, a sort of flying bicycle, called a Flicycle.

'Hmm, Hmm,' said Polly. 'That's all very interesting, but we really must get on with our rescue operation!'

'Quite right, my dear, quite right!' agreed the wizard. He tottered off into a back room, muttering snatches of spells, and clicking his fingers. Polly paced up and down impatiently while Wizard Idea emptied drawers out, searching for his tools.

At last he returned with a hammer, a saw and some nails. Eventually, he managed to restore the magic staff almost to its former shape. They tied a ribbon round it to hide the joins, and stuck a big star on the top, to 'pretty it up a bit' as the wizard put it.

'There you are, my dears, take it and off you go!' he said.

'Off *you* go? Do you mean you're not coming with us?' asked Polly.

'Good gracious me, no! I'm much too old and doddery. I can't get around like I used to! But don't worry, you'll be perfectly all right. Just bonk Haggis over the head with my magic staff and say the magic words.'

'That sounds quite easy, doesn't it, Polly? But what are the magic words?' asked Bloggs.

'Ah ... that's a point,' replied the wizard. 'Now, what were those magic words? I wrote them down only the other day. Now let me think ... Ah yes, Bescu ... Beribescu ... Oh no!'

Polly bit her nails anxiously. If only the

70

wizard would get a move on. Didn't he realise how precious time was?

After about half an hour of writing things down on pieces of paper, humming and haing, and crossing things out with a pencil stub, the wizard had patched together a strange little magic spell. It went like this:

> *'Bescu, Beribescu, Bazagra, Bedad!*
> *Stop the witch from being so bad.*
> *Bescu, Beribescu, Bazagra, Bezady!*
> *Turn her into a harmless old lady.'*

The Magic Bird, who had recovered from the journey by now, strongly advised Wizard Idea to have Haggis turned into something safe, like a frog or a toad. But the wizard said that would never do, as neither 'frog' nor 'toad' rhymed with 'Bezady'. They argued about this for quite some time, while poor Polly got even more desperate. But eventually it was settled, and Polly wrote down the spell so that she and Bloggs could learn it on the journey.

'This Flicycle of yours, does it really fly?' asked Bloggs.

'Does it fly!' exclaimed the wizard. 'It does just about everything! Swoops, dives, aerobatics and somersaults. Would you like a little spin in it?'

'Well, I was thinking,' replied Bloggs, 'that if your Flicycle really does work, it would be the most sensible way to get to Haggis' Castle, as time is getting short.'

Polly agreed enthusiastically, and Wizard Idea seemed only too pleased that his latest invention was going to have its first test run at last. He'd never been able to try it out because of his rheumatism.

He led the way across the snow to the garden shed, where he kept the Flicycle. It was green and yellow, with wheels and spokes everywhere, and two sets of long dragonfly wings along the side. They wheeled it out and Wizard Idea rushed round whirling propellors and pressing buttons. Polly oiled the pedals while Bloggs pumped up the tyres. They were all ready to go.

'Aren't you forgetting the magic staff?' came a chirpy voice. It was the Magic Bird again.

'Oh Magic Bird, thank goodness you reminded me! Whatever would I do without you?' said Polly, and she rushed back into the castle to fetch the staff. 'You are coming with us to Haggis' Castle, aren't you? I've never fought a dragon before, and I shall need your help.'

'If you don't mind, Polly,' said the Magic

Bird, 'would you let me stay with Wizard Idea for a while? I feel my part of the mission is over.'

'Of course,' said Polly warmly. 'Thank you for all your help. I'll send you a sack of birdseed when I've rescued Tom.'

She kissed the wizard goodbye. 'We'll send your staff back with the birdseed,' she promised. Tom would return the staff when it was all over.

At last, with a deafening creaking and back-firing, the Flicycle rose from the ground, and they were off! Bloggs pedalled furiously.

'Goodbye, goodbye!' called the old wizard. 'Now I know that my Flicycle works, I can start constructing my Pan-galactic Rollercoaster.' And he hobbled into the castle with the Magic Bird on his shoulder. He had already forgotten all about Polly and Tom.

9
The Final Journey

Everything was going wrong for Haggis. She'd tried pretending that Prince Tom was really a princess, but Zoro had taken one bite out of his shining armour, and broken his false teeth. He was furious about not getting the special birthday feast she'd promised, and swore never to help her with any spells again. Haggis was getting desperate, and when she was desperate she was dangerous.

She'd put Tom in a dungeon and tried to forget about him. But this wasn't easy, as Tom kept singing snatches of opera to cheer himself up. The noise was getting on Haggis' nerves.

Worst of all, she'd been watching Polly's amazing quest in her crystal ball. She'd never thought for one moment that anyone would actually go and get the magic staff back for the old wizard. It had seemed an impossible task for any ordinary person – but then it seemed this little busybody, Polly, was no ordinary person.

She must get that staff off Polly somehow. And she would destroy it once and for all this time, even if it was a difficult and dangerous process. Of course the staff was no use to a witch like her, because its fantastical powers only worked *against* evil. Until she had managed to steal it, Wizard Idea had been rushing about spifflicating all kinds of witches and warlocks, and ruining all their evil magic. It would have been her turn next, if she hadn't cunningly stolen it from the old spoilsport!

And now here was this tinpot princess charging through the night, hell-bent on bashing her over the head and shouting rude spells at her. It really was too bad!

'It's no fun being a witch any more!' she wailed. 'All the joy's gone out of wickedness nowadays! But just wait till I get my hands on that magic staff – what won't I do to that interfering little madam! I'll show her! No-one will be able to stop me then. I'll be chief witch of the universe! Boss of the world!'

This thought made her feel much better. She swigged down her tea and wrote out another list of evil plans and horrid surprises for Polly.

Meanwhile, Polly and Bloggs were not

having an easy time with Wizard Idea's Flicycle. It kept breaking down or getting punctures. Moreover, Polly was finding it increasingly difficult to hold on to the magic staff. When Wizard Idea had stuck the three pieces together again, it had seemed more like a homely, patched-up, old walking stick than anything else. But as time went on, the joints began to flow and meld together. The whole staff began to vibrate with a strange energy.

Then it started shimmering with an eerie supernatural glow of first violet, then red, blue and green rays. And the closer they came to Haggis' Castle, the fiercer the glow became. It shone and glimmered in the darkness, lighting their way through the night.

It was midnight when they reached Haggis' Castle, which was built on a squat crag surrounded by a moat. To get to the castle, one had to cross a rotting drawbridge, and climb up steep steps cut in the crag to the entrance. The castle lay silent and menacing under a pale moon.

But inside, Haggis was busy. She was just putting some finishing touches to a few nasty surprises for them.

She had persuaded Zoro to lie in wait on the drawbridge, with the promise that his birthday feast would be arriving soon, in person.

'But no eating,' Haggis had warned him, 'until you've got that staff off her.'

Zoro had agreed to let bygones be bygones, if he could only have a crunch of deliciously munchable princess again. So there he was, waiting on the drawbridge, when Polly and Bloggs arrived, wearily pushing the Flicycle.

The staff was shining brighter than ever now. The surrounding air seemed to hum with the energy that radiated from it. Zoro soon realised that Haggis had tricked him. The birthday feast had arrived, yes. But Haggis hadn't mentioned anything about dangerous-looking birthday candles. So, he was going to have to fight for his supper! He

gargled gently in the back of his throat and sent a jet of flames along the drawbridge at Polly and Bloggs.

'I like my princesses well cooked!' he called.

Polly's feet were singed by the flame. Bloggs hastily parked the Flicycle on the bank, but Polly stepped forward on to the bridge, holding the staff high.

Zoro quickly sent another spurt of flame at her, that sparked and crackled along the wooden planks.

'What's that you've got there?' he called. 'It looks dangerous. Put it down. Somebody might get hurt!'

Polly decided to call his bluff. She moved closer.

'It's a magic staff . . .' she paused. 'It's for turning dragons into harmless pussy cats!'

'That's close enough then. Stay where you are!' he replied. He tried to breathe out some more flames, but he had a bad cold, and all that came out was a muffled sneeze. So he flapped his wings and charged at them across the bridge. He rose clumsily into the air, knocking Polly over sideways so that the staff fell from her hands. Then he flew back and forth over their heads like a gigantic bat, clipping them with his claws and scaly wings whenever they tried to rise. But Polly managed to crawl towards the staff and grab it as it rolled backwards and forwards on the edge of the drawbridge.

The touch of the staff gave her new strength. It seemed to lift her to her knees. With tremendous force she swooshed it about above her head, hitting Zoro several times on his soft underbelly.

Zoro crashlanded astride the bridge, splintering the railings on either side. He was groaning with pain, but otherwise unchanged. Obviously it was not enough just to hit your enemy with the staff. You had to know the right spell. Wizard Idea had not mentioned any special spells for dealing with the dragon. Perhaps she could just change a few words of the other spell?

She went over to Zoro, chanting:

'Bescu, Beribescu, Bezagra, Bedad!
Turn this dragon into a . . .'

But Zoro had pulled his tail back on to the bridge and was limping hastily up to the castle before she could finish.

'Phew!' said Bloggs. 'Well done, Polly! There was a nasty moment when I thought we'd had our bacon!'

Then, suddenly, there was a creaking

sound and the drawbridge started to move upwards.

'Hold on tight to the side!' shouted Bloggs.

But as they clung to the railings, the bridge suddenly went down again with such a crash that they both let go and slid down to the end again. Then the bridge started upwards again without warning, until they were suspended dizzily over the moat below.

Polly looked down into the water. The surface was frothing and foaming. She realised with horror that there were live things in there – horrible squirming creatures with long, muscular tendrils that churned the water.

With the staff in one hand, she could barely hold on with the other. She felt her grasp slipping. The bridge jerked up, then suddenly down again. Polly felt herself hurtling downwards. In the seconds while she fell, she thought she could hear cruel laughter echoing round her.

The freezing water seemed to explode over her. As she fought her way up to the surface, some of the slimy water creatures slid strong tentacles around her, trying to pull her down. Others tried to wrest the staff from her grip. She forgot all about Prince Tom now. It was herself she was trying to save!

As she struggled back to the surface, she

heard Bloggs call out from the bank, 'Don't let go!'

Her only hope was for Bloggs to catch hold of the other end of the staff. But a scaly, snake-like tendril wound round her neck and pulled her under. She saw great eyes watching her beneath the surface. Somehow she imagined they were Haggis' eyes gloating at her. With one last desperate effort, she lunged upwards with all her might, flinging the staff up in the direction where she hoped Bloggs would still be.

No-one else could possibly have caught it, but Bloggs was a clown, trained in all the skills of the circus. He caught the staff neatly in one hand with the ease of a juggler. Then, using it as a spear, he plunged it down again and again among the thrashing tentacles in the dark water. The creatures slunk hastily back into the depths below. The waters became still once more.

Polly caught hold of the staff and Bloggs hauled her up on to the bank. Then he held her shivering body in his arms to warm her up.

He looked around to see if there was anywhere he could take her to dry off, and suddenly realised that they were on the castle side of the moat, on the bank that jutted out below the steep stairway cut in the cliff. That was something anyway. But Polly must rest before her next ordeal. He took off his striped jacket and put it round her.

But Polly hadn't forgotten her mission, and she felt more determined than ever to deal with Haggis once and for all, whatever the perils. She felt a sinking certainty that by now Tom must have been eaten or bewitched. Well, she would avenge his death, or meet her own with courage.

She opened her eyes and looked up at the castle high above them on the crag. She tried to remind herself that the wizard had said it

would be simple, that all she had to do was hit Haggis over the head and shout the spell. He hadn't warned her about dragons on drawbridges, water creatures and crags. He probably thought that after dealing with an ogre and a sorceress, she would know what to do. More likely of course, he'd forgotten altogether.

They set off up the stone steps. Polly was still shivering with cold, but the steep climb warmed her up. Suddenly a rock hurtled past them. Then another, and another.

'Look out!' shouted Bloggs. 'It's a landslide!'

'It's not a landslide!' Polly yelled. 'Look up there!'

In the moonlight, they saw the silhouette of Haggis, hurling rocks down at them, as easily as though they were dried peas.

They ran quickly to the shelter of a boulder.

'I wonder if the staff could help us. I'll just try something,' said Polly.

'Come back! It's too dangerous!' shouted Bloggs, but Polly stepped out with the staff. Down came another rock. Polly swung the staff like a cricket bat – WHAM! The rock hit the staff with a tremendous crack and went bouncing straight back up and through a

85

window in the castle. There was a loud splintering of glass. Then silence.

'If you think you're so clever, missy, try this lot!' shrieked Haggis. She sent a volley of assorted rocks, stones and tins of DAMSEL IN DISTRESS down on Polly. Some hit her, or bounced off nearby rocks; but some she whacked back up at Haggis. One tin hit Haggis on her hooked chin, making it even more crooked. Haggis leapt back, clutching her wound.

'Come up here then, if you dare!' she yelled, and retreated back into the castle, slamming the door.

10
An End to the Matter

Poor Polly was covered with bruises. Bloggs carried her up the last two hundred steps to the castle entrance.

'What on earth do we do now?' said Polly. Ringing the doorbell hardly seemed the right thing.

'Come on out, Haggis!' called Bloggs.

'Come inside!' came a voice through the letter-box, frighteningly close.

The great door swung open. In fear and trembling, holding the staff between them, they entered the dark castle and found themselves in a huge hall.

The staff burned fierce and brilliant, throwing vast shadows along the walls. Polly and Bloggs gasped and jumped back in dismay. There, on the opposite wall, they saw a gigantic shadow, with high-pinnacled hat and ragged arms outstretched – the dreaded Haggis herself!

For an awful moment Polly thought the

fifty-foot-high shadow was the enemy she must fight, and her heart failed her. Then the terrifying shadow swooped downwards, and Polly saw below, on the floor, the real Haggis bend to pick a flaming torch from a stand.

'Welcome to my castle, Polly dear!' she said. 'As you can see, I've been expecting you. I see you've enjoyed the fun and games I laid on, but now it's time for business.'

She threw the torch into a large cauldron. It flared up instantly, and Haggis' green face was illuminated horribly in the light.

'It has to be a nice, large cauldron, you see, to fit in all three of you. You, your funny friend there, and that ridiculous staff thing of Wizard Idea's.'

'The game's up, Haggis!' returned Polly. 'We've come to rescue Prince Tom and punish you, once and for all!'

'Prince Tom? Oh yes, that reminds me. Prince Tom left you this in his will.' Haggis brought out Tom's helmet and sent it clattering along the floor. 'He gave me this as a souvenir.' She held up his gold watch and chain, and began to swing it slowly backwards and forwards.

'You look tired, dear. Yes, I can see your eyelids drooping. You're falling ... falling ... asleep!'

'Don't listen, Polly! She's trying to hypnotise you!' whispered Bloggs.

But Polly was staring in a trance at Tom's gold watch, already falling into Haggis' power.

'By the time I count up to ten, you will be fast asleep. You will walk over here with the magic staff, and you will place it in the cauldron. Then you will be in my power!'

Polly began to move across the hall in a death-like trance. She held the staff before her; her face was white in the ghostly light it shed. Her lips moved, but no sound came out.

Bloggs, despairing, ran before her, slapping her, pinching her, begging her to wake from her trance. But nothing could halt her slow progress to the cauldron.

Haggis crooned delightedly, 'That's right, dearie, that's right! Throw it in here.'

She stood by the cauldron. Polly was close to her now. Bloggs was dancing up and down, shouting, in a last attempt to rouse her. Polly slowly raised the staff in the air.

'That's lovely. Now drop it in!' crowed Haggis excitedly.

But Polly brought the staff down with tremendous force on to Haggis' head, chanting aloud the magic spell that Wizard Idea had taught her:

'Bescu, Beribescu, Bazagra, Bedad!
Stop the witch from being so bad.
Bescu, Beribescu, Bazagra, Bezady!
Turn her into a harmless old lady.'

There was a flash of green lightning round the hall, and Haggis leapt up screaming, 'I don't want to be harmless ... I don't want to be good! I want to be wicked and nasty and bad! I want ... I want ...'

She suddenly stopped and scratched her head. 'Sorry, what was I saying? Oh yes ... I want to be a nice, kind, harmless old lady! I've always wanted to help other harmless old ladies cross roads ... to take thorns out of pussies' paws . . . to be kind to little children.'

Haggis put her arm round Polly and led her into the kitchen, saying, 'You look a bit dazed, dear. A nice cup of tea is what you need.' Somehow the staff must have miraculously protected Polly from the witch's hypnotic spell.

Bloggs, too, was feeling quite dazed. He followed Polly and Haggis into the kitchen. Gently, he took the staff from Polly's grasp. It was dim now. All its magic was, for the moment, spent.

'Thank you so much, dear, for making me good,' Haggis was saying. 'Milk and two sugars? You know, I've been thinking. Wouldn't it be nice to start an orphanage for little children. I think I'll go on a sponsored broomstick ride to raise money for it! Yes, and Zoro shall help me.'

Polly sipped her tea, and felt her strength returning.

'And Tom?' she asked. 'Has he really been eaten?'

'Oh, you mean my lodger? What a considerate boy! Why bless you, no! He's in the guest room downstairs. Zoro will get the key for you. Zoro!' she called.

Zoro came out from the larder where he'd been hiding. Haggis made him apologize for all the trouble he'd caused. He was such a coward that, as soon as he saw Polly and the magic staff, he burst into tears, and swore to become a vegetarian, if Polly would promise not to turn him into a pussy cat. Polly was so relieved to hear that Tom was alive and uneaten that she forgave him, on condition that he helped Haggis with the sponsored broomstick ride.

Then Polly took the key and went downstairs to the dungeon. She opened the door. Prince Tom was lying, fast asleep, in a corner.

'Typical!' thought Polly. 'I slave away trying to rescue him, almost killing myself, and there he is, fast asleep!' She poked him, none too gently, with the staff.

Tom opened his eyes. 'Ah Polly, how lovely to see you again. I can't tell you what a terrible time I've been having!' He gave her a big kiss. 'All the same, I'm very glad that it was me that got kidnapped and not you. This is no place for a nice girl like you ... rats and spiders. You'd have lost your nerve completely.'

Polly laughed. 'Yes, I'm sure I'd have been terrified. But I expect you coped magnificently!'

'Well, it's all in a day's work for a knight in shining armour. Now that I'm free, though, let's rush off and get married straight away.'

'Ah, that reminds me,' said Polly, 'I've made some wonderful arrangements for the wedding feast entertainment!' She told him about Pandora's Magic Circus.

'A circus, eh? I see. While I've been rotting away in this horrible dungeon, you've been sitting at home worrying about the wedding arrangements!'

Polly just laughed again, and told him that, in fact, she'd been extremely busy rescuing him. Tom was amazed to hear of her exploits.

'Oh Polly,' he said, giving her a big hug. 'Did you really do all that for me?'

When they went back up to the kitchen, they found Haggis, Bloggs and Zoro all drinking large mugs of tea and eating waffles with jam, as if they were old friends. Bloggs had told Haggis all about the Flicycle and she persuaded him to swap it for her broomstick.

So that's how we'll leave them. Bloggs, Polly and Tom all mounted Haggis' broomstick and rode back to Pomerania for a slap-up wedding.

What a marvellous wedding it was! People are still talking about it today. Guests and entertainers came from all over the world. Even Wizard Idea managed to get down for the celebrations because, now that he'd got

94

his staff back, he could magic away all his rheumatism. But, undoubtedly, the star attraction of the whole wedding day was the wonderful circus. And, to everyone's delight, the bride and bridegroom were shot through the Human Cannon to their honeymoon, somewhere on the lovely Costa del Pomerania.

Of course, Bloggs never told Haggis what a hopeless invention the Flicycle had proved. He certainly didn't tell her that he and Polly had had to push it most of the way from the North Pole, on foot.

In fact, it's rumoured that Haggis and Zoro

are still wearily pushing it round the world on their sponsored ride to this very day. And if any of you have ever been round the world, then you'll know that it's uphill most of the way!